# KATIE KAZOO, SWITCHEROO

# On Your Mark, Get Set, Laugh!

by Nancy Krulik • illustrated by John & Wendy

Grosset & Dunlap

For Lauren and Alexandra, who
are headed down the right track!—N.K.

For Don—a real good sport!—J&W

Text copyright © 2004 by Nancy Krulik. Illustrations copyright © 2004 by
John and Wendy. All rights reserved. Published by Grosset & Dunlap, a
division of Penguin Young Readers Group, 345 Hudson Street, New York,
New York, 10014. GROSSET & DUNLAP is a trademark of
Penguin Random House LLC.
Manufactured in China

Library of Congress Cataloging-in-Publication Data

Krulik, Nancy E.
  On your mark, get set, laugh! / by Nancy Krulik ; illustrated by John &
Wendy.
      p. cm. — (Katie Kazoo, switcheroo ; 13)
  Summary: When fourth-grade Katie turns into her unfair track coach, she
gives all the kids on the team a chance to compete, including the slowest
runner in her class.
  ISBN 0-448-43605-1 (pbk.)
  [1. Track and field—Fiction. 2. Schools—Fiction. 3. Teamwork (Sports)—
Fiction. 4. Magic—Fiction.]    I. John & Wendy. II. Title.

  PZ7.K9416On 2004
[Fic]—dc22

2004005226

10 9 8 7 6 5 4 3 2 1

Proprietary ISBN 978-1-101-95135-4
Part of Boxed Set, ISBN 978-1-101-95128-6

# Chapter 1

"I . . . can't . . . run . . . much . . . more," Katie Carew huffed and puffed as she ran beside her friend Emma Weber.

"Me neither," Emma said, gasping for air. "This seems a lot longer than a mile!"

Katie agreed. Her legs felt like limp spaghetti. And she still had another lap to go.

Gym class sure had changed from last year. When Katie was in third grade, gym had been so much fun. The gym teacher let the kids play fun games like Steal the Bacon and Crab Soccer.

But now that she was a fourth-grader, things were different. For starters, gym wasn't called *gym* anymore. The new gym teacher, Coach Debbie, called it *physical education.*

Coach Debbie was tough on the fourth-graders. She wanted them all to be able to run a mile in ten minutes or less by the end of the year.

Mandy Banks and Andrew Epstein were *really* fast runners. They could already run a ten-minute mile. Emma Stavros, Kadeem Carter, and Kevin Camilleri had all almost made it.

Katie wasn't so fast. She and Emma W. were usually pretty far behind the rest of the class. But at least Katie wasn't last.

George Brennan always held that spot. He was the slowest runner in class 4A.

"Not bad, girls!" Coach Debbie told Katie and Emma as they crossed the finish line. She clicked her stopwatch. "You did that in fourteen minutes."

"That's a full minute faster than last time," Katie said, out of breath.

"But it's still not a ten-minute mile," Emma W. said. She bent over and rested her hands on her knees.

"Walk it off, girls," Coach Debbie told Katie and Emma. "We've got to wait for George to pull up the rear anyhow."

Katie looked out on the track. George sure seemed tired. He wasn't running anymore. He was walking the last lap.

"George needs to get new sneakers," Kadeem told the kids.

"Why?" Emma S. asked.

"Because right now he's just a *loafer*!" Kadeem chuckled at his own joke.

Katie didn't laugh. "Nobody can be good at everything," Katie reminded Kadeem.

"Yeah, but George isn't good at *anything*," Kadeem insisted.

"He is too!" Kevin leaped up to defend his best friend. "George is the funniest kid in the whole fourth grade. He would never have told a lame joke like that shoe one you just told."

Kadeem frowned. Katie knew that Kadeem thought he was the funniest kid in the fourth grade.

When George finally crossed the finish line, Coach Debbie clicked her stopwatch. "Eighteen minutes, George. Same as yesterday."

"At least I didn't do worse," he said.

"We'll get you in shape yet," Coach Debbie assured him.

George thought for a moment. "I guess I would do better if I had a cold."

"Why's that?" Coach Debbie asked.

"Because I'd have a racing pulse and a running nose!" He laughed really hard. So did everyone else in the class.

"See, I told you," Kevin told Kadeem. "George is the funniest kid in the fourth grade!"

Coach Debbie shook her head sternly. "Physical fitness is no laughing matter," she reminded the boys.

George and Kevin bit their lips to keep from giggling.

"Anyway, I have an exciting announcement!" Coach Debbie exclaimed. "It's track team season! Since you're in fourth grade now, you kids can be on the team. Fourth, fifth, and sixth-graders can join."

The kids all started talking at once. They were really excited.

"I have to warn you," the coach continued. "The kids on *my* track team will have to work hard! You've got to be physically fit if you want to beat the other schools."

"When are the tryouts?" Mandy asked.

The smile fell from Coach Debbie's face. "Cherrydale Elementary School does not allow tryouts for sports teams. Anyone who wants to can be on the team. That's Principal Kane's rule." She sighed and shook her head. "I have no choice but to do what the principal tells me to."

Katie was confused. Principal Kane's rule meant everyone had a chance to play for their school. But Coach Debbie did not seem happy about that. In fact, she seemed kind of angry. That was strange. Usually, teachers *wanted* kids to volunteer for things.

Obviously, Coach Debbie wasn't a usual kind of teacher.

# Chapter 2

When physical education was over, Katie walked back to her classroom with the rest of the kids. She was still pretty tired from all that running. She and Emma were the last ones in the door of room 4A.

"Check out Mr. Guthrie!" George shouted. "He looks like Abraham Lincoln."

Katie looked at her teacher. He was wearing a fake beard, a black jacket, and a stovepipe hat. Katie poked Emma in the ribs and laughed. Emma giggled at their teacher too.

Mr. Guthrie was always doing things like that. Just last week, Mr. Guthrie had dressed like King Tut for math class. He'd made the class build pyramids out of plastic bricks. Piling those bricks up just right was harder than Katie had thought.

Mr. Guthrie wasn't like any teacher Katie had ever had before. Especially not Mrs. Derkman!

Last year, in third grade, Katie's teacher had been Mrs. Derkman, the strictest teacher in the whole school. She had lots of rules in her classroom. The desks in her room were all in neat rows. And the kids had to sit in their assigned seats all year long.

That wasn't the way things were in Mr. Guthrie's class. For starters, there weren't any desks in class 4A. The kids sat in beanbag chairs and leaned on clipboards to do their written work.

Mr. Guthrie let the kids decorate their own beanbag chairs. During the first month of school, when they were studying birds, they'd turned their beanbags into nests.

Now, they were about to begin a history

project. So Mr. Guthrie had asked the kids to decorate their beanbag chairs to represent important periods in American history.

Katie was really proud of her design. Her beanbag looked like the first American flag. She'd glued a circle of thirteen white paper stars to her beanbag, and added red and white streamers to make stripes.

Emma W.'s beanbag was right next to Katie's. She'd built a cardboard model of the Statue of Liberty on her seat. Katie thought it looked amazing!

"I hope we get to be partners for the history project," Emma whispered to Katie as they sat down on their beanbags.

Katie nodded. "I hope so too."

Last year, Katie would have wanted either Jeremy Fox or Suzanne Lock for her partner. They were Katie's best friends in the whole world. But they weren't in Katie's class this year. They were in class 4B with Ms. Sweet.

At first, Katie had been sad that she wasn't in a class with her best friends. But it hadn't turned out so bad. Katie still played with Jeremy and Suzanne after school. And Katie and Emma had become really good friends, too.

"Check out George," Kevin told the class. He pointed toward George's beanbag.

George had decorated his seat to look like the rowboat George Washington had used during the Revolutionary War.

"Stroke! Stroke!" George called out. He was standing on his beanbag, pretending to be George Washington. "Hey, do you guys know why pictures of George Washington always show him standing?"

"Why?" Katie wondered.

"Because he would *never* lie!"

Everyone started to laugh . . . except Kadeem. He opened his mouth to tell a joke of his own.

But Mr. Guthrie stopped him. "Not now, dude," the teacher told Kadeem. "Save it. I'll let you guys have a joke-off later today."

Katie smiled. She loved George and Kadeem's joke-offs. They told their best jokes, and then Mr. Guthrie let the class vote on who was funnier. George had won the last joke-off, so Katie was pretty sure

Kadeem would have some great jokes today.

But for now, it was time to get to work.

"Okay, you guys, here comes the moment you've been waiting for!" Mr. Guthrie announced. "I'm going to assign history partners. You have to work together to come up with a topic. Then you have to plan and present an oral report."

Emma looked over at Katie and crossed her fingers.

Katie crossed her fingers too. Then she held her breath and waited.

# Chapter 3

"Okay," Mr. Guthrie began, "Mandy, you and George will be working together.

"Andrew, you and Emma . . ."

*Oh, no!* Katie gasped.

". . . Stavros," Mr. Guthrie continued, "are partners."

*Phew. Wrong Emma.*

"Now, Katie Kazoo, it's time for you," Mr. Guthrie teased, using the super-cool nickname George had given her. "You and Kadeem will be paired up for this one."

*This is horrible,* Katie thought to herself. *I wish . . .*

Katie was about to say that she wished she could have any other partner besides Kadeem.

But she stopped herself. Katie didn't make wishes anymore. She knew what could happen when they came true.

It had all started one day at the beginning of third grade. Katie had lost the football game for her team, ruined her favorite pair of pants, and let out a big burp in front of the whole class. That night, Katie had wished she could be anyone but herself.

There must have been a shooting star overhead when she made that wish, because the very next day, the magic wind came.

The magic wind was a wild tornado that blew just around Katie. It was so powerful that every time it came, it turned her into somebody else! Katie never knew when the wind would arrive. But whenever it did, her whole world was turned upside down . . . *switcheroo*!

The first time the magic wind came, it had turned Katie into Speedy, class 3A's hamster! That morning, Katie had escaped from the hamster cage and wound up stuck inside

George's stinky sneaker! Luckily, Katie had switched back into herself before George could step on her.

The magic wind came back again and again after that. Sometimes, it changed Katie into other kids—like Jeremy, Emma, and Suzanne's baby sister, Heather. One time, it even turned her into Mrs. Derkman. Katie had almost had to kiss the teacher's husband, Freddy. *That would have been so gross!*

Katie never knew when the magic wind would return. All she knew was that when it did, she was going to wind up getting into some sort of trouble.

That's why Katie didn't make wishes anymore. She didn't want them to come true.

The way Katie figured it, with Kadeem as her partner, she didn't need any more problems.

# Chapter 4

At three o'clock on Thursday, Katie and Emma raced out onto the field behind the school. They were very excited. Today was the first track team practice.

The fifth and sixth-graders were huddled together near a tree. Some of them were stretching their legs, getting ready to run.

Mandy, Jeremy, Kevin, and Andrew were practicing their long jumps. After each jump, they measured who had gone the farthest.

Katie and Emma walked over to where the fourth-graders were jumping.

"Hey, you guys," Jeremy greeted them. "Isn't this cool?"

Katie nodded, but didn't say anything. She was a little nervous.

"You know, last year the track team went for ice cream every time they won a meet," he continued.

Emma smiled. "Then I hope we win *every* meet," she said. "I can't get enough chocolate, chocolate chip!"

"I like cookie dough," Jeremy told her.

Just then, Suzanne came racing up to them. "Hi, guys!" She was wearing navy running pants and a matching sweat jacket. She looked like a real track star.

"I didn't know you liked running track," Jeremy said to her. "I thought all you cared about was that modeling class you take on Wednesdays."

"Running's okay," Suzanne admitted. "But I'm *really* here to hang out with fifth and sixth-graders! They hardly ever talk to us. So this is my chance."

Jeremy looked over to where the older kids were stretching. It didn't seem like they even noticed that the fourth-graders were there!

"They're *still* not talking to us," Jeremy told Suzanne.

"They will," Suzanne assured him. "They have to. *We're a team.* Look, here comes the coach now."

"Hello, track team!" Coach Debbie greeted them. "Are we ready for a winning season?"

"Yeah!" the kids shouted back.

"I can't hear you!" Coach Debbie said.

"Yeah!" The kids screamed louder.

"Great!" the coach said. "Because today,

you're going to work harder than you ever have before. You're going to discover muscles you never knew you had. It's going to be tough. But it's worth it. After all, you are the few, the proud, the Track Team!"

Katie gulped. Coach Debbie sounded more like a general in the army than a teacher.

"You have to be physically fit to win track meets. You've got to be ready for anything!" Coach Debbie continued. "Track meets are full of surprises."

At that moment, the team's *first* surprise arrived.

"Sorry I'm late!" George huffed as he ran onto the field. "It took me a while to tie my new sneakers." He held out his foot to show off his new running shoes.

Coach Debbie seemed more shocked than anyone to see George there. "*You're* joining the track team?" she asked him. She did not sound happy.

George nodded. "Sure. My dad was on the

track team when he was in high school. He
thought it was fun."

Coach Debbie turned red in the face.
"*Fun*? Track is not about fun! Track is about
winning! We are here to WIN! WIN! WIN! If
it weren't about winning, they wouldn't bother
to keep score."

George gulped. "Sorry," he said.

"You're going to be," Coach Debbie assured him. "Now drop and give me ten."

"Ten what?" George asked.

"I think she means push-ups," Katie told him.

"Exactly," Coach Debbie agreed.

Katie smiled proudly.

"And since you're so smart," Coach Debbie continued, "you can give me ten, too. In fact, everyone can. That's what happens on my team when someone arrives late to practice."

She lifted her silver whistle to her lips and blew . . . hard. "Okay, enough chitchat. One . . . two . . ."

"George, this is all your fault!" Suzanne said as she did her push-ups.

"Yeah, thanks a lot," Mandy added.

George's face turned red. Katie couldn't tell if he was embarrassed, or just having a hard time doing push-ups.

One thing was for sure, though. The track team wasn't nearly as much fun as she'd thought it would be.

# Chapter 5

On Friday morning, Katie was in pain.
Every one of her muscles was stiff because of
yesterday's tough track practice. She was not
in a good mood at all.

And working with Kadeem on the history
project was just making things worse.

"Here's a good topic," Katie suggested. The
class was in the library doing research for
their projects. She pointed to a chapter in one
of the history books. "We can do our report
on the first Thanksgiving. We could dress as
Pilgrims and . . ."

"Do you know what kind of music the
Pilgrims danced to?" Kadeem asked her.

Katie looked in the book. It didn't say anything about music. "No. What kind?"

"Plymouth *rock*!" Kadeem chuckled.

Katie laughed—a little. It was a funny joke after all. But there really wasn't time for fun. They had too much work to do. She stood up to get another book.

"Hey, where are you going?" Kadeem asked.

"To get another history book. We have to pick a topic."

"Speaking of picking," Kadeem said, "did you ever hear this one? You can pick your friends, you can pick your nose, but you should never, *ever* pick your friend's nose!" Then he picked up a paper airplane and threw it across the room.

*That was gross!* Katie had had enough of Kadeem. So instead of getting a new history book, she decided to walk over to Mr. Guthrie.

"Hey, Katie," he greeted her. "How's it going?"

"Terrible," Katie moaned.

"Anything I can do to help?" Mr. Guthrie asked.

"You can give me another partner for this project," Katie suggested hopefully.

"Sorry, kiddo. No can do," he replied. "Everyone's all paired up."

"Then I can work by myself," Katie volunteered. She looked over at Kadeem. "I'm sort of doing that anyhow."

Mr. Guthrie leaned back in his chair. "You're having a hard time working with Kadeem, huh?"

"He's not working at all!" Katie cried out. "I can't get him to agree to any topic. I tried lots of ideas, like the Revolutionary War, the first Thanksgiving, even a biography of Abraham Lincoln. Nothing interests him."

"Oh, something must interest him, Katie," Mr. Guthrie said gently. "Everyone has interests."

"Not Kadeem."

Mr. Guthrie laughed. "Sure he does. And if

you think hard enough, I'm sure you'll figure out what they are."

Katie sighed. Teachers were always doing things like that. They would tell you that the answer was easy. All you had to do was look for it. But they would never tell you what that answer was.

"History isn't just wars, presidents, and important events," Mr. Guthrie continued. "Sometimes, it's told through the lives of ordinary people and the things they liked to do."

"Huh?"

Mr. Guthrie smiled. "You'll make it work. I know you will. There's nothing Katie Kazoo can't do!"

Katie looked back toward Kadeem. Instead of reading a history book, her partner was busy tying his own shoelaces together.

She wasn't so sure.

# Chapter 6

After school, Katie and some of her pals went to practice running in Katie's backyard. They wanted to be ready for the big track meet next week.

"Coach Debbie said that on Monday, she'll let us know what races we'll be in," Jeremy told the others. "She's going to post a note on the bulletin board outside the gym."

"I hope I'm in the relay race," Emma said. "I think it's better to be part of a group. That way, if I'm slow, someone else who's fast can help our team catch up."

"I want to jump over the hurdles," Suzanne added. "I've got the perfect legs for it—long,

thin, and muscular."

"I can jump over hurdles too," George said. He leaped up into the air, and spread his legs too.

*THUD!* George landed right on his rear end. "Ow, my aching butt!" he moaned.

The kids all started giggling. George laughed right along with them. That was George—he would do anything for a laugh.

*But at least he knows when to be serious,*

Katie thought to herself. *Not like Kadeem.*

"Maybe we should run a few laps," Jeremy suggested.

Katie nodded. "Everybody ready?" she asked.

Suzanne held out her foot so everyone could see her red-and-white running shoe. "My new sneakers are ready to go!"

"So are mine," George said. He held out his foot too. "My dad got me these. They're supposed to make you run like the wind."

"Cool," Jeremy told them. "Then let's run."

Jeremy took the lead, running quickly in circles around Katie's yard. Suzanne, Emma, and Katie all followed behind him.

As usual, George was the slowest of anyone. But Katie could tell he was really trying.

*BOOM!* Just then, George fell . . . again. *This* time, he landed right on his belly.

"Oops," he groaned as he picked himself up. "I tripped over my new shoelace."

"You ran more like a rock than the wind," Suzanne teased him.

"I don't know why I joined the stupid track team," he said. "I stink."

"No, you don't," Katie tried to tell him.

"Well . . ." Suzanne began to disagree, but the look in Katie's eyes made her stop.

Just then, Pepper, Katie's chocolate-and-white cocker spaniel, ran over to George. *Slurp.* He licked him right on the mouth.

"Blech!" George said, wiping the dog spit from his lips. "What did he do that for?"

"It's his way of telling you that you can do it," Katie told him.

"You can't give up," Emma added.

George didn't seem so sure. "I'm a lousy runner," he told them. "I always get tired before I can finish."

"Maybe you're better at running *short* distances," Jeremy suggested. He pointed to the pine tree across the yard. "Let's see how fast you can run from here to that tree. I'll set my stopwatch."

"Okay," George said.

"On your mark," Jeremy called out. "Get set. Go!"

George ran as fast as he could.

"Ruff! Ruff!" Pepper took off after him. He reached the tree *way* before George did.

"Oh, man," George complained. "Even Katie's dog can beat me."

"He's got four legs instead of two," Katie reminded George. "That makes him twice as fast."

"Maybe we should get Pepper to join the track team," Jeremy joked. "He could be our secret weapon."

"Well, Coach Debbie *did* say that anyone who wanted to could be on the team," George agreed.

"I think you have to be a student at the school, though," Emma said.

George shrugged. "We'll dress him in little doggie jeans and put a hat on his head. Mr. Guthrie will never know he's a dog."

Katie laughed at the thought of Pepper sitting in her classroom, barking out answers to Mr. Guthrie's questions. "George, you crack me up," she told him.

"Wait until you see me in a race," George told her. "I'll really make you laugh then." He started to run again. This time, he made his legs look all wobbly and goofy.

Katie laughed even harder. So did Emma, Suzanne, and Jeremy.

"I hope Coach Debbie has as good of a sense of humor as we do," Suzanne whispered to Katie.

Katie frowned. Somehow, she didn't think so.

# Chapter 7

On Monday morning, Katie went with her class to the school library. They were supposed to work on their history projects. Everyone was excited to find information on their topics.

Everyone but Katie and Kadeem, that is. They didn't even *have* a topic yet.

Katie went to the history section of the library and pulled a few books off the shelves. "Here," she said, passing two books to Kadeem. "You look through those, and I'll look at these."

Kadeem opened the cover of one of the books. Then he yawned and closed it again. "This stuff is boring," he said.

"You think the Civil War is boring?"

"It is to me."

Katie sighed. "Well, then how about the California Gold Rush?"

"What's that?" Kadeem asked.

Katie slid a book over to him. "Here, read about it."

"Why don't you just *tell* me?"

But Katie was tired of doing all the work. "Read it," she demanded. "Stop being lazy!"

"I don't feel like it," he told her.

"You don't feel like doing *anything*!" Katie said, banging her fist on the table. "What's wrong with you?"

All the kids stared at Katie.

"Keep your voice down, please," the library teacher said.

Katie hadn't meant to be loud. It was just that she was so frustrated with Kadeem!

Kadeem looked angrily at Katie. "I'm out of here!" He got up and raced out of the library.

Katie followed Kadeem out of the library.

"Go away," Kadeem said, once they were alone in the hallway.

"I'm sorry," Katie told him. "I didn't mean to upset you. I just wanted *you* to read the book for a change."

"Yeah, well, that book's really hard," Kadeem blurted out.

"It's not that hard . . ." Katie began. Then she stopped. "Oh my goodness. Can you read, Kadeem?"

"*Of course* I can read," Kadeem said proudly. Then he frowned. "Just not that well."

"Oh."

"Hey, it's not like I'm stupid or anything," he assured Katie. "I have a learning disability. It makes it hard for me to read. But I'm working with a tutor. I'm getting much better."

"That's good," Katie replied. Now she felt awful for yelling at Kadeem.

"Doing research in books takes me a really

long time," he continued. "I wish I could listen to a tape or watch a video instead. I remember *everything* I hear. One time, I watched this TV show with stand-up comics. I memorized every joke they told."

"Wow!" Katie exclaimed.

Kadeem frowned. "But that doesn't help us."

Katie thought for a moment. Suddenly, she got one of her great ideas. "Maybe it does," she said slowly.

"Huh?"

"I think I've got a great topic for us! But we're going to have to get some help from Mr. Guthrie." She grabbed Kadeem by the hand. "Come on. This is going to be so much fun!"

# Chapter 8

Katie was in a great mood after the library. She ran out to the playground for recess.

"Hi, Suzanne!" Katie shouted to her best friend.

"Katie, isn't it awful?" Suzanne said with a frown.

"What?"

"About the track meet," Suzanne told her. "Didn't you see the note Coach Debbie posted?"

Oops. Katie had been so excited about her history project that she'd totally forgotten about the track meet. "What's wrong? Was it canceled?" she asked Suzanne.

"No. Not for everyone. Just for us," Suzanne said angrily.

"What do you mean?"

"Coach Debbie is only letting the best runners compete. Andrew and Mandy are running in the relay race with two sixth-graders. Jeremy is running in one race and throwing a shot put. The rest of us fourth-graders are on the bench."

"That's not fair," Katie said. Her good mood was fading fast.

"I know," Suzanne agreed.

"There must be some mistake," Katie began.

Suzanne shook her head. "It's not a mistake. I saw it with my own eyes."

"We have to talk to Coach Debbie," Katie insisted.

"What for? She doesn't want to let us compete."

Katie took Suzanne by the hand and dragged her to the gym. "Come on," she insisted.

×　×　×

Coach Debbie was putting away basketballs when Katie and Suzanne walked into the gym. "Hi, girls," she greeted them. "Excited about our big meet on Thursday?"

"No," Suzanne answered.

"Uh, well, actually, that's what we're here to talk to you about," Katie said. "How come we're not running?"

"There are only a few races. I didn't have enough spaces for everyone," Coach Debbie explained.

"Jeremy's running *and* throwing the shot put," Suzanne told the coach. "Evan and Rachel from the fifth grade are running in two races. And that sixth-grader Maya is doing the long jump *and* the relay race."

"Well, *those* kids are really . . ." Coach Debbie began. Then she stopped herself. "Look, there are plenty of track meets this season. There's time for you to compete. For now, just think of yourselves as cheerleaders for the team."

Suzanne cocked her head to the side.

"Cheerleaders," she said. "Okay." A slow smile formed on her face.

Katie looked at her friend strangely. Suzanne had given in awfully quickly . . . for her, anyway. There had to be a reason why.

So what was it?

# Chapter 9

"Okay, team, it's time to crush the competition!" Coach Debbie shouted as the track team gathered on the field. Of course, she was only talking to the few kids who were actually competing. She pretty much ignored the rest of them.

Suddenly, Suzanne raced onto the field.

"Wow!" Emma exclaimed, looking at Suzanne.

"What's she supposed to be?" a fifth-grader named Sophie asked.

Katie looked at her friend. Suzanne was wearing a bright red and white sweater and a short red skirt. And she was carrying red and white pom-poms. Suzanne was a cheerleader!

"Go, team! Go, team!" Suzanne shouted.

"Where did you find that uniform?" a sixth-grader named Lauren asked her.

"At the mall. It's red and white . . . our school colors."

"I didn't know we had school colors," George said.

"We do now," Suzanne told him. She shook her pom-poms right in his face.

Katie laughed. Now she knew why Suzanne had been so happy to be a cheerleader instead of a runner. She was getting more attention this way. Suzanne *loved* attention.

"We've got that spirit!" Suzanne cheered. "Come on, let's hear it."

But Coach Debbie wasn't thinking about

school spirit. She had only one thing on her mind. "We've got to WIN! WIN! WIN!" she shouted to the team. "Do whatever it takes. Just win!"

Katie was shocked. A teacher was supposed to tell the team to have fun and play fair. But Coach Debbie hadn't mentioned any of that.

Just then, the referee blew the whistle. It was time for the first race.

"That's me!" Jeremy told Katie.

"Good luck!" Katie said.

"Break a leg," Suzanne added.

Coach Debbie turned red in the face. "Why did you say that?" she demanded.

Suzanne gulped. "All I said was to break a leg. It's what actors say to wish each other luck."

"This *isn't* a theater," Coach Debbie reminded her. "It's a track meet. How can we WIN! WIN! WIN! if one of our best athletes has a broken leg?"

Suzanne looked like she was going to cry. "I'm sorry," she apologized.

"You should be," Coach Debbie said. Then she turned to Jeremy. "Get out there and pulverize the competition!"

✕ ✕ ✕

Jeremy did what Coach Debbie asked. He won, won, won his race!

"Wow!" Katie congratulated him. "You did it!"

"I was afraid not to. Coach Debbie would have been mad. Boy, is she scary!"

The two friends looked at their physical education teacher. She was jumping up and down beside the track.

"WIN! WIN! WIN!" Coach Debbie yelled as some sixth-graders ran a relay race. "You have to WIN! WIN! WIN!"

✕ ✕ ✕

Sure enough, Cherrydale Elementary School won their first track meet! It was very exciting. Especially when they all got to go out for ice cream.

"Next week, I want you guys to run even faster," Coach Debbie told the kids. "I want you to cause some major damage. Crush the competition. WIN! WIN! WIN!" She threw her hands up in the air. Her scoop of chocolate ice cream flew off the cone and landed on the ground with a splat! But Coach Debbie didn't seem to care.

George rolled his eyes. "She's going crazy," he whispered to Katie.

"Maybe it's because this was our first meet," Katie

replied. "I'm sure she'll be calmer next week."

"I hope so," George said. "I don't want to run if she's going to yell at me."

"We won't get to run," Kevin complained. "She's never going to give any of *us* a chance."

"Sure we will," Katie said. "Coach Debbie said there would be lots of chances for everyone to race. I'll bet anything that next week it will be our turn."

# Chapter 10

When Coach Debbie posted a new list of runners for the next track meet, Katie's name wasn't there. Neither were Suzanne's, Emma's, George's, or Kevin's. The same kids who had run races last week were running again.

"This just isn't fair," George complained as he sat down on the grass next to Katie. "I don't know why I even came to this track meet."

"I could be spending my time working on my history project," Emma said. "I still have a lot of research to do."

"I'm quitting this team," Kevin said. "Who's with me?"

Katie thought about that for a moment. She and Kadeem still had work left to do on their project. But Kadeem had volunteered to do research by himself while Katie was at the track meet. He was really into it.

Still, Katie did sort of feel like she was wasting her time being at the track meet. But she wasn't a quitter.

"We can't quit," Katie said. "Not yet. It's only the second track meet. I'm sure things will get better. Maybe if we talk to Coach Debbie and ask her for a chance. She did promise Suzanne and me that . . ."

Katie didn't get to finish what she was saying. She was drowned out by Suzanne's cheering.

"Thunder, thunderation," she cheered. "We're the best team in the nation!"

Suzanne seemed really happy. It would be nice if Katie could have felt that way too. But Katie didn't really want to cheer. She wanted to run a race. Unfortunately, it didn't look like that was going to happen today.

Just then, Coach Debbie began to scream. "Oh, no! This is awful!" She stared at a note in her hand. "Maya has the flu! She's our best runner. We can't beat Apple Valley without her!"

"Can't someone else run her races?" Jeremy asked the coach.

Katie stood up and began jogging in place. She hoped Coach Debbie would see how much she wanted to WIN! WIN! WIN!

That was a great idea. Coach Debbie *did* notice her! "Katie," she called out. "I need you to run . . ."

"I'm ready!" Katie interrupted eagerly. "Which race?"

"Race?" Coach Debbie asked, confused. "Oh, no. I was going to ask you to run and get a bottle of cold water for *Evan*. He's going to compete in the long distance race Maya was supposed to run."

"But Evan is already running two races,"

Katie reminded the coach.

"I know," Coach Debbie replied. "That's why he needs more water. Now go, Katie. Hurry. The team is counting on you!"

Katie couldn't believe it! Now she was *really* mad. Coach Debbie was so mean! All she cared about was winning! She shouldn't be a teacher at all.

That was it! After today, Katie decided she was going to quit the team.

The gym was empty when Katie arrived. She hurried toward Coach Debbie's office, where the refrigerator was. Suddenly, she felt a cool breeze on the back of her neck.

Katie looked around. The nets on the basketball hoops weren't moving in the breeze. The papers on Coach Debbie's desk were completely still.

The breeze only seemed to be blowing around Katie.

Oh, no! This wasn't an ordinary wind. This

was the magic wind! It was back. And there was nothing Katie could do to stop it!

*Whoosh!* The magic wind picked up speed. It swirled wildly around Katie. It was powerful and out of control. Katie was really scared.

But she was even more scared when the wind *stopped* blowing. She knew what that meant. The magic wind was gone . . .

And so was Katie Carew.

# Chapter 11

Katie opened her eyes slowly and looked around. Wow! That had been some strong wind. It had blown Katie right out of the gym. Now she was standing in the middle of the track field.

Okay, so now she knew *where* she was. But she still didn't know *who* she was.

"Coach Debbie!" she heard Evan shout. "Do you want me to run this race for Maya?"

There was no answer. Katie looked around for the coach. She didn't see her anywhere.

"Do you want me to run now?" Evan asked again. Then he gave Katie a funny look. "Are you okay, *Coach Debbie*?"

Katie gulped. Evan had been talking to *her*! Slowly, she looked down at her body. Katie wasn't wearing her lucky cocker spaniel T-shirt anymore. Instead, she was wearing a shirt that said "Winners Never Quit." She had a silver whistle hanging around her neck. And her own red sneakers had been replaced with a pair of very white, very large running shoes.

*Coach Debbie's* running shoes!

Oh, no! Katie had turned into Coach Debbie. Right in the middle of the big meet! This was *so* not good.

*Or was it . . . ?*

Just then, Katie got another one of her great ideas. "No, Evan," she told him. "I think you've run enough. It's time to give someone else a chance." She turned to Kevin. "You run in this race."

"Huh?" Kevin asked.

"I said, 'Run this race,' " Katie repeated. She tried to sound strict. Just like the real Coach Debbie.

Kevin was shocked. But he wasn't going to give up his chance to run. "Okay!" he shouted excitedly as he ran for the starting line.

As soon as the referee said, "Go!" Kevin took off like a shot. He ran the fastest he ever had.

"Suzanne, go cheer for him," Katie told her best friend. "Show him we have spirit. *Lots of spirit!*"

"Sure, Coach!" Suzanne agreed. She leaped up and ran toward the track.

"Let's go, Kevin!" she cheered as she waved her pom-poms wildly.

Katie grinned. Things were going great . . . until Suzanne threw her pom-poms high in the air. She managed to catch one of them. But the other pom-pom flew off in the direction of the track. It landed right on Kevin's head! He couldn't see.

Kevin got all turned around. *He started running in the wrong direction!*

"No, Kevin!" Katie shouted. "That way!"

Kevin stopped, whipped the pom-pom from his face, and spun around. But it was too late. He'd lost the race.

"Suzanne! What did you do?" one of the sixth-grade boys shouted.

"I can't believe you made him lose!" a fifth-grade girl added.

Suzanne looked like she was going to cry. This wasn't the attention she wanted from the older kids. "Coach Debbie told me to cheer!" she swore to them. "It's all her fault."

Katie frowned. It was the truth. She *had* been the one to tell Suzanne to cheer. What a mistake that had been.

But there was nothing Katie could do about it now.

"Look, you guys," she said finally. "It's just one race. Besides, winning isn't everything."

The kids stared at her in amazement.

"Coach Debbie, are you sick or something?" Rachel asked her.

Katie shook her head. "Sure, winning is great. But so is teamwork, and fun! *That's* what this team should be about."

She looked at her clipboard. "Okay, the next race is the hurdles. Suzanne, you're perfect for this."

Suzanne gulped. "Me?" she asked nervously. "But I've never jumped over a real hurdle before."

"You can do it. You've got long, strong legs. Like a racehorse."

Suzanne gave Katie a look. Katie knew that Suzanne probably didn't like being compared to an animal. But she also knew that she wasn't going to argue with her coach. Not when she was actually giving her a chance to run.

"Okay." Suzanne started to run toward the track.

"Uh, Suzanne?" Katie stopped her.

"Yes?"

"Leave the pom-poms back here."

Suzanne dropped her pom-poms and hurried off to the starting line.

As soon as the referee blew his whistle, Suzanne ran as fast as she could to the first hurdle. She cleared it easily.

Suzanne was doing really well! Katie was so happy. If Suzanne won this race, the kids would forget about what had happened with Kevin and the pom-poms.

More importantly, it would prove that other kids could WIN! WIN! WIN! too.

Suzanne took the next hurdle just as easily. But the third one was much higher. Suzanne had never jumped over anything that tall. She leaped up into the air, and . . .

"Ouch!" she cried out as her knee hit the wooden hurdle. Suzanne flipped over onto the ground. Her skirt flew up in the air. Good thing she was wearing shorts under her skirt! Otherwise everyone would have seen her underpants. How embarrassing would that have been? It was bad enough that she'd lost the race!

"Hey, Coach," Evan said as Suzanne walked back over toward the team. "Next time you want to put that horse in for a race, I vote *neigh*!"

Suzanne looked like she was about to cry.

# Chapter 12

Unfortunately, Katie couldn't take the time to make her best friend feel better just then. There was still one more race to run.

"The next race is the relay," Katie told her team. "Emma, you're going to take the first lap."

Emma seemed a little surprised. So did the rest of the kids.

Next, Katie turned to Annabelle, a tall, thin fifth-grader who was a fast runner. She could help the team if Emma fell behind. "Annabelle, you take lap number two. Rachel, you're third. Mike, you take fourth, and . . ."

Katie looked around for a minute, trying

to find just the right person to finish the relay. "And for the final lap, how about . . ." She took a deep breath. *"George."*

Everyone gasped. *Especially George.* "Not me, Coach! I'm always last!"

"You're getting better every day," Katie reminded him. "I have faith in you."

"I wish *I* did," George said. He looked at his teammates. "I'm sorry . . . in advance."

✕ ✕ ✕

"On your marks. Get set. Go!"

As soon as the referee blew his whistle, Emma ran as fast as she could down the track. Katie had never seen her friend's legs move so quickly.

"Go, Emma!" Katie shouted excitedly. "You can do it. Try your best!"

The kids all stared at her.

"What happened to 'Win! Win! Win!'?" Rachel asked Kevin.

Emma kept up the pace. But the first Apple Valley relay runner was quick. She pulled ahead of Emma early on, and never lost the lead. By the time Emma passed the relay baton to Annabelle, Apple Valley was way ahead.

Luckily, Annabelle was a super speedy runner. She soon caught up to the Apple Valley runner. They were practically tied as they came around the bend.

Katie's heart began to pound. Rachel would be next, and then Mike. They were both really fast runners. It looked like Cherrydale Elementary had a chance to win the relay!

Then Katie remembered something: *George was the last runner in the relay.*

Suddenly, it didn't seem like such a great idea to have George run. He was probably going to lose his part of the race. And if he did, Apple Valley Elementary would have enough points to win the whole track meet.

"I can't look," Katie groaned.

As Annabelle handed her baton to Rachel,

Katie turned and ran off to hide behind a thick tree at the other end of the field. Katie couldn't see a thing. The track team couldn't see her either.

In the distance, she heard kids cheering loudly. Katie hoped it was her team cheering. Suddenly, she felt like she really *was* Coach Debbie. She wanted to win that badly.

But the real Coach Debbie would have pulled George out of the race. And Katie would never *ever* do that.

Suddenly, a fiercely cold wind began to blow. Katie pulled Coach Debbie's sweat jacket tight around her. The leaves on the trees were still. The grass wasn't moving either. Katie knew right away that this was no ordinary wind. This was the magic wind!

The magic wind grew stronger and stronger. It whirled around Katie like a tornado. Faster and faster it blew, until the wind was so strong, Katie could barely breathe.

And then it stopped. Just like that. The magic wind was gone.

Katie Kazoo was back!

Of course, that also meant that Coach Debbie was back too. And Katie had a feeling she wasn't going to be too happy to see George in the race.

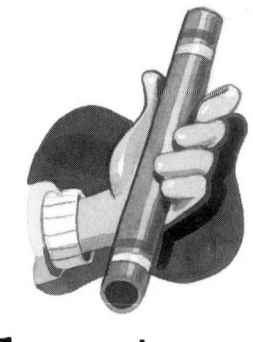

# Chapter 13

"George, what are you doing? Get back here!" Coach Debbie shouted as she ran over to the starting line.

"But you told me to run this race," George told her.

"I did not . . ." Coach Debbie said angrily. She stopped for a minute. She was very confused. "I mean . . . I would never put you . . . at least I don't think . . ."

"You said he could run the last lap. We all heard you," Kevin insisted.

Coach Debbie frowned. "But . . . I . . . wouldn't . . . would I? Oh, I don't know what I did." She seemed confused. But only for a moment. "However, I *do* know this," she said firmly. "I'm pulling you out now!"

"You can't do that," the referee told Coach Debbie. "Once he's standing by the starting line, he has to run the race. It's the rule."

"Oh, no. We've lost this one," Coach Debbie moaned.

George frowned. He felt terrible.

Katie felt badly too. All she'd wanted to do was give her friend a chance to run. But George wasn't ready for such a big challenge.

And now everyone was going to be mad at him for losing.

Katie looked out at the track. Mike had just started to run his lap. He was way in the lead. Cherrydale could have a chance—if George could pull it together enough to win his lap.

Suddenly, Katie had another one of her great ideas. Sure, George wasn't as fast as the Apple Valley runner. But he had something the other kid didn't.

She ran over to the starting line. "George!" she shouted.

"Go away," George said sadly.

"No. Listen. Here's what you gotta do," she said. "Make him laugh."

"What?"

"Make him laugh," Katie repeated. "He can't run fast if he's laughing."

George's eyes lit up. "Hey, that's right!" he said excitedly.

As soon as George grabbed the baton from Mike, he took off down the track. But he didn't run like the other kids did. Instead, George made his legs wobble and wiggle. He twirled around like a ballerina. Then he leaped up in the air and did a goofy clown-like split.

"Check him out!" an Apple Valley kid said.

"He's so funny!" another agreed.

Everyone was laughing at George. Sam, the boy running for the Apple Valley team, turned around to see what was happening. He began to chuckle too. He couldn't help it.

"That's it, George!" Katie shouted to him. "It's working! Now run!"

George ran as fast as he could. He actually caught up with Sam!

"Tell him a joke!" Katie yelled to George.

"You know who the best runner in history was?" George asked between huffs and puffs.

Sam couldn't believe George was asking him questions in the middle of a race. He stared at him in amazement.

"Adam," George joked. "He was first in the *human* race!"

Sam started to laugh again.

Now George began to run faster than he ever had before. As he pulled ahead of Sam, he left him with one last joke. "You know how fireflies start a race? On your marks! Get set! Glow!"

Sam giggled so hard that he had to bend over and hold his belly. That left the track wide open for George. A few moments later, he crossed the finish line way ahead of Sam.

George had led Cherrydale Elementary School to victory!

The Apple Valley coach stormed over to Coach Debbie. "Your team cheated," he shouted at her. "That kid made my runner laugh."

Coach Debbie shrugged. "I don't see anything in the rule book against that. Can I help it if your runner can't concentrate on the race?" Coach Debbie answered. "My team WON! WON! WON!"

The Apple Valley coach looked angry. But Coach Debbie was right. George had been sneaky. But he hadn't cheated.

As the other coach stormed off, Coach Debbie looked at George. "Well, you did it," she told him.

"Thanks for putting me in, Coach," George grinned. "That was fun."

"It's not about f . . ." Coach Debbie began. Then she thought about it. "I guess it *is* about fun," she admitted. "And that was very clever of you."

"Thanks," George said, taking a bow. "But it was all Katie's idea."

"Well, it isn't going to happen again," the coach continued.

"That's not fair!" Katie shouted out. "Even kids who aren't the fastest runners should be allowed to try."

Coach Debbie nodded. "I agree. I didn't say George wasn't going to run any more races."

"What do you mean?" George asked her.

"I'll put you in again, but you'll have to win on your sports ability. Not your jokes."

George frowned. "I don't have a chance."

"Sure you do," Coach Debbie assured him. "There are other competitions besides relay races at a track meet. I liked that split you did in the air. With a little work, you could be a top-notch hurdle jumper."

Suzanne frowned. That was definitely not *her* talent.

"I'm not sure what happened here today," Coach Debbie continued, "but George reminded me of something I'd forgotten a long time ago. The best way to win at anything is with teamwork. You guys have different talents. We need to use them all."

George leaped in the air and spun around like a crazy ballerina. "I'm ready!" he teased.

# Chapter 14

"Okay, Kadeem, this is it," Katie announced on Monday morning. They were standing out in the hall, waiting to go into the classroom and do their history presentation.

"It's all under control," Kadeem assured her.

Katie smiled. Kadeem had turned out to be a pretty cool partner. He was smart, and really creative too. In fact, the costumes for their presentation had been his idea. They were really wild.

Katie was wearing a big box around her body. On her head, she wore a hat with a hanger glued to it. That was supposed to be her old-fashioned TV antennae.

As Katie walked into the classroom, the kids all pointed at her and laughed. But she didn't care. That was the whole point of dressing like a TV set!

"Our report is on the history of TV comedies," Katie told the class. "We watched lots of old videos to see what the first TV shows were like. We found out that the first big TV star was a funny guy named Milton Berle. People called him Uncle Miltie." She turned toward the door.

Kadeem entered the room. He was wearing a dress!

"Check out Kadeem!" Andrew giggled.

Kadeem curtsied low. He fell over onto the floor.

The kids laughed.

"Uncle Miltie wore goofy dresses and hats on his TV show, to make people laugh," Kadeem told everyone. "He was especially good at a kind of comedy called slapstick.

That's when the actor falls down, bangs his head, or does other silly things just for a laugh."

"I think his *face* is good for a laugh," Katie told the class. "Don't you?"

The kids all stared at her. They couldn't believe she was saying something so mean, right in the middle of her history presentation!

Kadeem walked to the corner of the room and picked up a huge whipped-cream pie. He and Katie had hidden it there earlier.

"You wouldn't dare," Katie said, staring at the pie.

Kadeem winked at the class.

*Bam!* Kadeem smashed the pie . . . *right in his own face.*

The kids in the class laughed really, really hard. They hadn't expected that!

"That's the kind of comedy people watched on old-fashioned TV shows," Kadeem explained as he licked the cream from his chin.

Katie laughed along with everyone else.

Kadeem was hysterical. She was so lucky to
have the two funniest kids in the fourth grade
in her class.

Suddenly, Katie felt something cold and
wet hit her right on the nose. It felt like a
gooey kind of rain. She looked around the
classroom. It didn't seem to be raining on
anybody else.

Oh, no! Had the magic wind returned? Was it bringing rain or hail with it now? Was it going to change her into someone else, right here, in front of her whole class?

Some of the wet stuff dripped into Katie's mouth. *Yum!* It hadn't been the magic wind at all. It was whipped cream. Kadeem had thrown a handful of it at her when she wasn't looking.

Katie was really glad she was going to be herself for a while. Especially when there was pie around. "Mmm . . ." Katie giggled as she scraped some pie off her cheek and tasted it. "Banana cream. My favorite!"

# Spice up Your Sneakers

George and Suzanne were really proud of their new sneakers. But Katie and Jeremy had been wearing the same old sneaks for a long time. Their running shoes had started to look run-down. Luckily, they knew exactly how to fancy up their footwear. Now you can too!

Just be sure to get your parents' permission before you start.

**You will need:**

| | |
|---|---|
| A pencil | Newspaper |
| Glitter | Your sneakers (of course!) |
| Fabric paints | |

# Friends for Never

by Nancy Krulik • illustrated by John & Wendy

Grosset & Dunlap

For Isabelle and Ian Gale—makers of
rainbows, with insatiable imaginations!—N.K.

For Eric—true friends for EVER!—J&W

Text copyright © 2004 by Nancy Krulik. Illustrations copyright © 2004 by
John and Wendy. All rights reserved. Published by Grosset & Dunlap, a
division of Penguin Young Readers Group, 345 Hudson Street, New York,
New York, 10014. GROSSET & DUNLAP is a trademark of
Penguin Random House LLC.
Manufactured in China

Library of Congress Cataloging-in-Publication Data

Krulik, Nancy E.

Friends for never / by Nancy Krulik ; illustrated by John & Wendy.

p. cm. — (Katie Kazoo, switcheroo ; 14)
Summary: Snubbed by her best friend Suzanne, Katie magically turns into
her as she is making her modelling debut at a fashion show at the mall.
Includes a recipe for fruit salad.
ISBN 0-448-43606-X (pbk.)
[1. Models (Persons)—Fiction. 2. Best friends—Fiction. 3. Friendship—
Fiction. 4. Schools—Fiction. Magic—Fiction.] I. John & Wendy. II.
Title. III. Series.

PZ7.K944Ft 2004
[Fic]—dc22

2004009203

10 9 8 7 6 5 4 3 2 1

Proprietary ISBN 978-1-101-95135-4
Part of Boxed Set, ISBN 978-1-101-95128-6

# Chapter 1

"Yodel-ay-hee-hoo!" Katie Carew shouted. "Yodel-ay-hee-hoo!"

"That was perfect!" her teacher, Mr. Guthrie, congratulated her. "You sounded like a real native of Switzerland."

Katie blushed. She wasn't usually the type of kid to yodel in front of her whole class. But that was the kind of thing you did when you were in Mr. Guthrie's fourth-grade class.

Mr. Guthrie wasn't a typical teacher. He did things his own way.

Like now. The kids were studying world geography. But rather than just reading about Switzerland, the kids in class 4A were standing

on a hill in the field behind the school, practicing yodeling. The hill was the closest thing the elementary school had to the mountains of Switzerland. Mr. Guthrie called it the Cherrydale Alps.

"Who's next?" Mr. Guthrie asked.

"Oh, oh, oh!" Kadeem Carter raised his hand really high. "My turn! Please, Mr. G.!"

Mr. Guthrie laughed. "Okay, Kadeem, let's hear *your* best yodel."

"YODEL-AY-HE-HOOOOOOOOOOOOOO!"

Katie covered her ears. So did a lot of the other kids. Kadeem was really loud.

Mr. Guthrie smiled. "That was definitely the yodel to beat all yodels."

Kadeem bowed to the class. "Thank you, thank you!" he said.

Katie rolled her eyes. Kadeem was always joking around.

"Okay, since nothing's going to top that, let's head back into the building," Mr. Guthrie said. "We have just enough time before lunch

to take a surprise math quiz."

"Ugh," the kids groaned. They hated surprise quizzes.

Katie sighed. Sometimes Mr. Guthrie could be just like any other teacher.

Katie walked into her classroom, plopped down into her beanbag, and got ready to take

the quiz. The kids in 4A all sat in beanbag chairs. Mr. Guthrie thought kids learned better when they were comfortable.

The kids were very proud of their beanbags. They spent a lot of time decorating them. The decorations reflected what the class was learning about.

When the class had been studying birds, the kids had all turned the beanbags into giant nests. When they had been learning about American history, the kids had used construction paper, glue, and cardboard to create historical scenes on their beanbags.

Right now, class 4A's world geography unit was Europe. Katie had used black pipe cleaners to build the Eiffel Tower from France on her beanbag. Her pal Emma Weber had constructed the London Bridge out of cardboard.

Emma Stavros had decorated her beanbag with pictures of funny-looking trolls from Norway.

Andrew Epstein's beanbag was the scariest one. He'd used cardboard and black construction paper to build a dark castle. His beanbag was supposed to be Dracula's home in Romania. There was even a picture of a vampire on the top of the castle.

George Brennan's beanbag was really goofy. He'd used lots of Styrofoam cups to build Italy's Leaning Tower of Pisa. In real life, that tower tilted a little to one side. On George's beanbag, the tower leaned so far over, it hit the floor. He was constantly gluing the cups back together.

Kadeem had a funny beanbag, too. He'd used brown cloth pillowcases stuffed with cotton to make a giant hot-dog bun around his red beanbag. He said it was a German frankfurter.

"Hey, Kadeem and Andrew," George called out. "You guys know what Dracula's favorite snack is?"

Kadeem shook his head.

"A fang-furter!" George said. He laughed at his own joke.

Kadeem couldn't let George be the only funny one. "What do you call a slice of dessert in Italy?" he asked.

"What?" George wondered.

"A pizza pie!"

Katie giggled. She really liked when George and Kadeem tried to out-joke each other. Mr. Guthrie called it having a joke-off.

"Wow," Mr. Guthrie exclaimed. "It's an international joke-off! Those were good ones, guys."

"Good enough to get us out of that math quiz?" George asked hopefully.

"Not a chance."

As Mr. Guthrie went to his filing cabinet to get the quiz, Katie thought about life in class 4A. Sure, they had to do regular work, like this quiz. But they also did a lot of really great stuff, like yodeling and telling jokes.

And the kids in class 4A were the only

ones in the whole school to have a *snake* for a class pet. No hamster, guinea pig, or turtle could *ever* be as cool as Slinky the Snake!

It was hard to believe that Katie had ever wanted to be in class 4B with Ms. Sweet. Not that Ms. Sweet wasn't a nice teacher. She was. But Mr. Guthrie was a lot cooler.

Then again, Katie's two best friends, Jeremy Fox and Suzanne Lock, were in class 4B. Katie missed them sometimes. It would have been nice to be with them all day.

But Katie still got to see Suzanne and Jeremy at recess, during track team practices, and on the weekends after her Saturday morning clarinet lessons. They still had lots of fun together.

Katie had learned something really important in fourth grade. She didn't have to be with her best friends all day long. No matter what class they were in, Katie and her pals were *friends forever*!

# Chapter 2

"Hey, Katie," Emma W. called as Katie walked out onto the playground after lunch. "You want to jump rope with Mandy and me?"

"Sure," Katie agreed happily. "Just let me find Suzanne. She's probably with Jessica. We can all play."

Katie knew Emma W. would like it if they all played together. Last year, when Emma was in class 3B, Jessica had been her best friend. But this year, they were in different classes. Emma didn't get to hang out with Jessica all the time anymore.

"Okay," Emma W. said. "But hurry up. I

have a new rhyme I want to try."

Katie looked around the playground for Suzanne and Jessica. She found them standing next to the big oak tree.

"Hi, you guys," Katie said as she approached Suzanne and Jessica. "Wanna jump rope with Emma W., Mandy, and me?"

Suzanne sighed. "Jump rope?" she asked. "Are you kidding?"

Katie seemed surprised. "Kidding?"

"We don't do that kind of stuff," Suzanne declared. Jessica nodded in agreement.

"But you jumped rope all the time last year," Katie reminded Suzanne.

"Exactly," Suzanne replied. "In *third* grade. But we're in fourth grade now. Jumping rope is for babies."

"Oh," Katie said. She felt embarrassed. She hadn't thought of it that way. "So what are you guys going to do?"

"Just hang out here and talk," Suzanne replied.

Katie frowned. She had to get back to where Emma and Mandy were waiting for her. They needed at least three people to play jump rope. "I don't really have time to talk," she said.

"That's okay," Suzanne replied. "Our conversation is private anyway."

Katie couldn't believe it! Suzanne, *her best friend*, was telling her to go away. She glared at Suzanne.

"Don't look so angry," Suzanne told her. "It's not about you. It's about my modeling class."

"What's so private about that?" Katie asked her. "Everyone knows you're taking a modeling class."

"Yes, but she's my new assistant." Suzanne pointed to Jessica.

"Your *what*?"

"I'm going to need an assistant when I'm a famous model," Suzanne explained to Katie. "So I have to teach her all about modeling stuff. That's what we're talking about. We've started a modeling club."

"What kind of stuff do you do in a modeling club?" Katie asked.

"Oh, you know, talk about new hairstyles and lip glosses." Suzanne stuck out her bottom lip. "I'm wearing grape gloss with glitter."

"Oh, I thought you ate a purple Popsicle at lunch," Katie said.

Suzanne rolled her eyes. "That's why *you're* not my assistant," she said.

"That was really mean, Suzanne," Katie replied.

Suzanne paused for a moment. "Oh, I guess I forgot to tell you . . ." she began.

"Tell me what?"

"My name's not Suzanne anymore."

Katie stared at her. "Excuse me?"

"Suzanne is too plain a name for someone like me. So I gave myself a new one. Now my name is Ocean. That's *much* more sophisticated."

Katie started to laugh. Suzanne had done some pretty weird things, but this was one of the weirdest! She looked over at Jessica. "What's *your* name? Sand?"

"Her name is *River*," Suzanne said. "I came up with it."

Jessica nodded. "Now we're Ocean and River."

"Water names, get it?" Suzanne added.

Katie looked at Ocean and River. They were in the same class. They'd given themselves new names. And they were in a club together—a club they had not asked Katie to join! They were acting like . . . *best friends*!

Katie knew she should get back to Mandy and Emma, but she didn't want to be left out by Suzanne and Jessica either. "Do you think

*I* should get a new name, too?" she asked. "I could be Sea or Waterfall or something."

Suzanne shook her head. "Plain old Katie fits you just fine. *You* don't need a sophisticated name."

Katie wasn't jealous anymore. Now she was just mad. "I'm not plain!" she exclaimed. "I'm as sophisticated as you are!"

Suzanne looked at Katie's red high-top sneakers and jeans. Then she studied her own black-and-white cowboy boots and short denim skirt. "Oh, Katie," she said. "Don't be silly. You're not sophisticated. You're just Katie."

Katie scowled.

"All the people in class 4A are pretty much like you," Suzanne continued. "You fit in just fine there. So it's okay."

Katie turned on her heels and stormed off. She wasn't going to talk to Suzanne about this anymore. *It wasn't okay.* Not at all!

# Chapter 3

That afternoon, Katie walked home from school all by herself. Emma W. had to help her mother take her little brothers for haircuts. Jeremy had a drum lesson. And *Ocean* was hanging out with River.

Katie felt really alone. She started to think about how things were in third grade—*back when she and Suzanne did things together.*

"I wish . . ." she began. Then she stopped herself, quick. Katie knew better than to wish for things. Wishes sometimes came true. And that could cause big problems.

It had all started one day at the beginning of third grade. Katie had lost the football

game for her team, ruined her favorite pair of pants, and let out a big burp in front of the whole class. It was the worst day of Katie's life. That night, Katie had wished she could be anyone but herself.

There must have been a shooting star over-head when she made that wish, because the very next day the magic wind came.

The magic wind felt like a wild tornado. But this wind blew just around Katie. It was so powerful that every time it came, it turned her into somebody else! Katie never knew when the wind would arrive. But whenever it did, her whole world was turned upside down . . . switcheroo!

The first time the magic wind came, it had turned Katie into Speedy, class 3A's hamster! That morning, Katie had escaped from the hamster cage and wound up in the boys' locker room! Luckily, Katie switched back into  herself before any of the boys could tell she was running around wearing nothing but

Speedy's fur coat.

The magic wind came back again and again after that. It had turned her into Lucille the lunch lady, Principal Kane, and even Katie's third-grade teacher, mean old Mrs. Derkman! One time, the wind switcherooed Katie into her science camp counselor, Genie the Meanie. That time, she'd gotten all her friends lost in the woods!

The wind had also changed Katie into other kids—like Emma W. and Suzanne's baby sister, Heather. One time, the wind had switcherooed her into Jeremy, and Katie had started a huge fight between all the girls and boys in her grade.

Another time, the magic wind had turned Katie into her very own dog, Pepper. She'd gotten into an argument with a squirrel and destroyed her next-door neighbor's garden. Considering the fact that Katie's next-door neighbor was Mrs. Derkman, it had been really awful.

Katie never knew who the magic wind was going to change her into next. But she did know one thing. She wasn't ever going to make another wish, ever again. Wishes didn't always turn out the way you expected them to.

# Chapter 4

The next morning, when Katie got to school, she spotted Suzanne walking back and forth in front of a tree. Her back was really straight and her neck was stretched up long, like a swan's. She looked kind of weird.

At first, Katie didn't want to go over and talk to Suzanne. She was still kind of mad at her about the day before.

Then she thought about it for a moment. She and Suzanne had been in fights before. But they always made up. Katie was pretty sure that Suzanne would be sorry about how she'd treated her yesterday. She would surely ask her to join the modeling club today.

Katie decided to give Suzanne another chance. That was the kind of thing best friends did for each other.

"Hi, Suzanne," Katie greeted her.

"*Ocean,*" Suzanne reminded Katie.

"Oh, yeah. Ocean. Hi."

"Hi." Suzanne kept on walking back and forth.

"What are you doing?"

"Practicing walking."

Katie looked at her strangely. "You've been walking since you were two."

Suzanne rolled her eyes and sighed. "I'm practicing walking on a *runway*, Katie," she explained. "I have a big modeling show coming up, remember?"

Katie nodded. "I think you walk really nicely," she assured Suzanne.

Suzanne frowned.

"*Nicely* isn't good enough. I have to be perfect. I want to be the model everyone remembers!"

At just that moment, Emma Stavros came running over to the girls. She was wearing a huge silver medal around her neck.

"Wow! Where'd you get that?" Katie asked. She was really impressed.

"At the ice-skating competitions yesterday. I took second place in figure skating!" Emma sounded really proud of herself.

Suzanne stopped walking and looked at Emma. "Only *second* place," Suzanne sniffed.

"Well, the first-place winner was a *sixth*-grader," Emma said with a shrug.

"Second place is awesome," Katie assured her. "And your medal is so cool! I've never seen one that big!"

"Thanks," Emma said with a smile. "Oh, look, there's Mandy. I've got to show it to her!"

"What a show-off," Suzanne said as Emma raced off toward Mandy.

Katie tried really hard not to laugh.

Imagine Suzanne calling someone *else* a show-off. "She's just proud. She should be. That's an amazing medal."

"It's tacky and ugly," Suzanne argued.

"That's what you say," Katie told her. "*I* think it's really cool."

"You don't know *anything* about accessories," Suzanne replied. "Someone as small as Emma S. should never wear a big silver medal around her neck."

Katie looked at her strangely. "What are you talking about?"

"*Accessories*. You know—necklaces, earrings, scarves," Suzanne explained. "I'm an expert on accessories. We're studying them in modeling school now."

Katie was getting tired of hearing about modeling.

But Suzanne wasn't finished talking about it. She looked Katie up and down, and then frowned. "You know, now that we're not in the same class, you don't dress as well as you used to."

Katie looked down at her black running pants and zebra-striped sweater. She liked the way she looked. "What's wrong with what I'm wearing?"

"It's the animal print," Suzanne told her. "That's *so* last year. This year, people are wearing different kinds of patterns. See?" She pointed to the pink, green, and yellow polka-dot shirt she was wearing.

Before Katie could reply, Jessica came walking over. "Hi, Ocean," she greeted Suzanne. "Hi, Katie."

"Hi, River," Suzanne said with a smile. Then she turned back to Katie. "You see the plaid skirt River's wearing? That's the kind of pattern I mean."

"Ocean helped me pick it out," Jessica

explained to Katie. "Our modeling club went on a field trip to the mall."

"We had fun, didn't we?" Suzanne asked Jessica. The girls giggled together.

Katie scowled. Obviously, Suzanne wasn't going to ask her to join their club after all.

"Did you bring the orange lip gloss?" Suzanne asked Jessica.

Jessica nodded. "And your round brush, too. Now you'll be able to fix your makeup and hair all day long."

Suzanne sighed heavily. "It's so much pressure being a model. I have to be gorgeous all the time."

*Ugh!* Katie couldn't stand listening to Suzanne's bragging anymore. She turned and walked away without even saying good-bye.

Ocean and River didn't even seem to notice she'd gone.

# Chapter 5

That afternoon, Katie and Emma W. walked home with Jeremy. As they left the school yard, Katie saw Jessica and Suzanne standing by themselves, giggling about something.

Katie frowned. "Those two are getting to be real snobs," Katie moaned.

"Getting to be?" Jeremy said. "Katie, Suzanne's always thought she was better than everyone else."

Katie sighed. She guessed that was true.

"She's *your* best friend, not mine," Jeremy reminded her.

Katie sighed again. These days, Suzanne

wasn't acting like she was Katie's best friend, either. "You know," she said slowly, "*we* could start a club. The three of us could be the first members."

"What kind of club?" Jeremy and Emma asked at once.

"Well, you guys know I take cooking classes on Wednesdays, right?" Katie asked.

Emma and Jeremy nodded.

"I know lots of great recipes now," Katie continued. "We could start a cooking club. I know my mom would let us meet in my kitchen."

"That sounds good," Jeremy agreed.

"It sounds *delicious*," Emma added.

"We could ask all our friends to join," Katie said. "Especially the ones who like to eat. We could meet Saturday afternoons, right after my clarinet lesson."

"We have to ask George, for sure," Jeremy said. "He'll eat anything. And Kevin will come if we're making something with tomatoes."

"He ate twenty-seven of those grape tomatoes at lunch today," Emma added. "I thought he was going to be sick."

"Not the tomato king," Katie assured her. "Kevin's eaten more than that before." She thought for a minute. "We should probably ask Mandy, Zoe, and Miriam, too."

"How about Manny?" Jeremy said.

"Sure," Katie agreed. "And Becky . . ."

"Do we have to ask *her*?" Jeremy interrupted. "She makes me nuts."

Katie laughed. Becky Stern had a big crush on Jeremy. She flirted with him all the time. He hated it.

"I think we should invite everyone," Katie said. Then she looked back to where Suzanne and Jessica were huddled together, talking. "Well, *almost* everyone," she corrected herself.

# Chapter 6

"Please pass the applesauce," Katie asked Mandy. She put a slice of cheese on top of each of her slices of bread.

It was Saturday afternoon. Katie, Mandy, George, Jeremy, Emma W., and Manny were all gathered in Katie's kitchen. They were making applesauce recipes from the recipe Katie had gotten in her Wednesday afternoon cooking class.

"This is a great idea," George said as he poured a heaping spoonful of cinnamon and sugar over the applesauce that he had plopped on a slice of bread. Then he put another slice of bread on top to make a

sandwich and covered it with a slice of American cheese. "Here you go, Mrs. Carew."

Katie's mother laughed as she popped George's cheese, applesauce, and cinnamon sugar sandwich into the oven. "That's your *third* sandwich, George," she remarked. "You must really like these."

"I love when the cheese gets gooey in the oven," he replied. "And the way the cinnamon and sugar gets all syrupy. Yum!"

"Oops!" Emma W. exclaimed. A big blob of applesauce had fallen on the floor. "I'm sorry, Mrs. Carew."

"Don't worry about it," Katie assured her friend. "Our cleanup crew will get it."

Sure enough, Pepper, Katie's cocker spaniel, padded over and began licking the applesauce off the floor.

"That dog will eat anything, Katie Kazoo!" George exclaimed, using the super-cool nickname he'd given her.

"Look who's talking," Jeremy said.

"George, I saw you put hot sauce on a tuna fish sandwich the other day. *Blech*!"

"I love hot sauce," George boasted. "The hotter the better. I'll eat it on anything."

"Even these applesauce and cheese sandwiches?" Manny asked.

George frowned. "Okay, well, maybe not *any*thing," he admitted.

Manny turned to Katie. "I'm going to start a database of all our recipes," he told her. "What do you think we should call these?"

Katie thought for a minute. Her friends all seemed really happy making the sandwiches. That gave her an idea. "How about Apple-y Ever After Sandwiches?"

"Perfect," Manny said. He took a pen from his pocket and wrote that down on the top of his hand. Manny was always writing things on his hands. That way, he never forgot anything—at least not until he took a shower.

"Katie, I can't believe you didn't ask Suzanne to join this club," Mandy said

between bites of her Apple-y Ever After Sandwich. "You guys always do things like this together."

"Not anymore," Katie replied.

"But you invited everyone else in our grade to join the club," Manny reminded her.

"Not everyone," Emma W. corrected him. "We didn't ask Jessica, either."

"They're too busy with their dumb old modeling club to do anything with us," Jeremy added.

"Look at me . . . I'm a model," George said. He wiggled his hips wildly, pretending to walk up and down a fashion runway.

The kids all laughed. At first, Katie felt kind of bad about the way George was making fun of Suzanne. Especially since she wasn't there to defend herself.

But then Katie remembered *why* Suzanne wasn't there.

"Aren't you and Suzanne friends anymore?" Mandy asked. She took a big bite of her

gooey applesauce sandwich.

Katie shrugged. "I guess not. She and Jessica, I mean *River*, do everything together now."

"But I thought you and Suzanne were best friends forever," Mandy continued.

Katie frowned. She was tired of hearing about Suzanne, or Ocean, or whatever her name was. "Well, now we're FRIENDS FOR NEVER!" she exclaimed loudly.

Everyone grew quiet. Katie's mother stared at her, surprised, but Katie knew her mom wouldn't say anything while Katie's friends were around.

Katie took a deep breath. She hadn't meant to sound so angry. Now everyone seemed really uncomfortable.

Katie wanted everyone to keep on having a good time. She forced herself to smile and held up her sandwich. "Here's another one for the oven, Mom."

After the cooking club had left, Mrs. Carew went outside to get the mail. She returned with a big handful of letters.

"Katie, there's one for you," she said as she walked in the door.

Katie jumped up from her seat. She *loved* getting mail. "Who is it from?" she asked excitedly.

"Suzanne."

"Oh," Katie said. "You can throw it out then."

"You don't even know what's in here," Mrs. Carew told her. She opened the envelope. "Oh, look, it's an invitation to Suzanne's modeling show. It's this Saturday at the mall."

Katie folded her arms across her chest. "I'm not going to that thing."

Mrs. Carew put her arm around Katie. "I know you're angry at Suzanne right now," she began gently.

"Her name's *Ocean*, remember?"

"That's *so* Suzanne," Mrs. Carew laughed.

Katie groaned.

"The thing is, you won't *always* be mad at her," Mrs. Carew continued.

"Yes, I will," Katie insisted.

"I doubt it," Mrs. Carew assured her. "You two have been friends for a very long time

and are always having fights. And you always make up."

"Well, not this time. And I'm not going to that dumb fashion show," Katie told her mother.

"Yes, you are," Mrs. Carew said firmly. "Suzanne has worked hard in this class. You need to be there to show your support for her."

"Why?"

"Because Suzanne cared enough about *you* to invite you," Mrs. Carew reminded her.

Katie had a feeling that Suzanne's mother had sent the invitation. But she knew better than to tell her mother that. It would be a waste of time. Once Mrs. Carew made up her mind about something, there was no changing it.

Katie folded her arms and slumped back into her chair. She was going to have to go to Suzanne's dumb old modeling show.

But that didn't mean she had to like it.

# Chapter 7

On Monday morning, Katie got to school just before the morning bell rang. Most of the fourth-graders were already in the yard, running around and playing tag.

Suzanne and Jessica were standing all by themselves. They were putting on lip gloss and fixing their hair.

As Katie walked by, she heard them talking.

"Dabba-id yabba-oo sabba-ee Babba-ecky's jabba-eans?" Suzanne said.

"Yabba-uck!" Jessica answered.

Katie looked at them strangely. "Did you say something?" she asked.

Suzanne shook her head. "Not to you. You

wouldn't understand."

"It's our secret code," Jessica answered. "Just for people in our club."

"So you two are the only ones who speak the language?" Katie said. She knew she was being mean, but she couldn't help it.

Jessica ignored Katie. Instead she turned her attention to Ms. Sweet, who had just walked onto the playground. "My mom gave me a note to give to *our* teacher," she told Suzanne. "I'll be right back."

"We're the only two members of the club for now," Suzanne told Katie as Jessica ran off. "But we've invited other people to join."

"You have?" Katie asked. "Who?"

"No one you know," Suzanne admitted. "We've sent invitations to all the top modeling agencies. We want real models in *our* club," she explained. "I'm sorry we couldn't invite you, but we don't want kids to be members."

"But you two *are* kids," Katie reminded her.

"Only for now," Suzanne replied. "We're

growing up quickly."

Katie frowned. "Yeah, well, your new language isn't so hard. All you did was stick the sound 'abba' in after the first letter of every word."

Suzanne gasped. Katie had figured out their code!

"I know what you said," Katie continued. "You asked, 'Did you see Becky's jeans?' and

Jessica answered, 'Yuck.' You guys are really, really mean!"

"We're not mean," Suzanne told her. "We're just fashionable. Can we help it if we're so much trendier than the rest of you?" She flipped her hair and turned her back on Katie.

"I can't believe we were ever best friends," Katie snapped. "Suzanne, you and I are FRIENDS FOR NEVER!"

Suzanne turned around quickly. "I think that's a *great* idea!" she responded angrily.

"Well, at least we agree on something!" Katie said as she stormed away.

Katie wanted to try and cool down after her big fight with Suzanne. But she wasn't going to be able to do that in her classroom. It was hot—*really hot*—inside the classroom. The air was very steamy. There were fake trees and flowers all over the place. The sounds of birds chirping and rain filled the

room. As usual, something really strange was going on in there.

"Here we go again," Kadeem said with a laugh.

"I guess we aren't studying Europe in world geography anymore," Emma S. added.

"Good guess!" Mr. Guthrie exclaimed as he jumped out from behind a big plastic tree.

"Ah!" Katie gasped. "You scared me."

"There's nothing to be afraid of here," Mr. Guthrie said.

"Where's *here*?" Kevin asked. He looked up at a monkey-shaped balloon in a plastic tree.

"We're in the Brazilian rain forest!" Mr. Guthrie announced.

Katie looked up and spotted the monkey-shaped balloon in the tree. Then she saw the vines that hung from the ceiling. The room really did look like a rain forest—except for the blackboard, of course. Suddenly, she wasn't all that jealous of Suzanne and Jessica anymore. All they had was a dumb modeling

club. Katie and her class were traveling to Brazil! (Well, sort of.) She smiled for the first time that day.

"It's really hot in here," Mandy said, fanning herself. "I'm sorry I wore a sweatshirt today."

"I can fix that," Mr. Guthrie said. He reached into a big plastic bag and pulled out a pile of T-shirts. They were all different colors. Each one said *Welcome to Brazil.*

"Girls, go change in the girls' locker room. You guys can put your shirts on in here. Then we can start talking about ways you can decorate your beanbags, so you fit into the rain forest landscape."

"Boy, Slinky sure looks happy," Kevin said as he looked into the snake's tank.

"This kind of warmth is perfect for a reptile," Mr. Guthrie explained.

Emma W. laughed. "It isn't great for hair, though," she said. "Mine's getting all limp." She wiped her bangs away from her forehead.

"And mine's curling up," Emma S. added.

All that talk about hair made Katie remember Suzanne again. Katie knew exactly what she could do to get back at her for being such a snob. "We should get Suzanne to come in here," she told the others. "She hates it when her hair frizzes."

"The rain forest just isn't fashionable," Emma W. joked.

"No, but it sure is fun," Katie agreed. She took a bright pink shirt from the pile. "I love these T-shirts."

"But, Katie, those shirts aren't in style." George imitated the snooty way Suzanne had been talking lately.

"They are in class 4A," Katie answered. "Everyone's wearing them!"

# Chapter 8

Class 4A's week in the Brazilian rain forest zoomed by. Before Katie knew it, it was Saturday—the day of Suzanne's modeling show.

"I have to work today," Mrs. Carew told Katie as they gulped down a quick breakfast. "And Dad's playing tennis. So I'll drop you off at the fashion show. You can meet me at the store after the show is over."

Katie nodded. Her mother was the manager of the Book Nook, a bookstore in the mall. The store was right next to Katie's favorite restaurant, Louie's Pizza Shop.

"Can I get a veggie slice at Louie's after

the show?" Katie asked her mother. "I'll have earned it by then."

"Sure." Mrs. Carew smiled kindly at Katie. "You never know, today could be more fun than you think."

"I doubt it," Katie said as she put on her jacket and headed out the door to the car.

When Katie got to the mall, she saw that a big stage had been set up in an open area. In front of the stage, Katie spotted Suzanne's parents sitting in the second row with Suzanne's little sister, Heather. Katie figured she should walk over and say hello.

"Hello," Katie said to Suzanne's parents.

"Hi, Katie," Mrs. Lock said.

"Hey there, kiddo," Mr. Lock said.

"Katieeeeeeeeeeeeeee!" Heather squealed. She took her thumb out of her mouth and gave Katie a big wet kiss.

Katie grinned as she wiped the baby spit from her cheek. She'd kind of missed Heather.

"We haven't seen you in a while," Mrs. Lock said. "How do you like fourth grade?"

"It's fun," Katie said.

"Suzanne's having a good time, too," Mrs. Lock said.

"Not today, she's not," Mr. Lock reminded his wife.

Katie looked at him. "What's wrong with Suzanne?" she asked.

"She's just a little nervous, that's all," Mrs. Lock assured Katie.

"A *little*?" Mr. Lock disagreed. "She's more than a *little* nervous. This morning, she told me she'd forgotten how to walk!"

Katie giggled. "I think she meant she forgot how to walk like a model."

Mr. Lock shrugged. "She walks fine as far

as I'm concerned."

Mrs. Lock sighed. "Katie, do you think you could go backstage and talk to her? You always calm Suzanne down."

"I don't think she . . ." Katie began.

"She'd be really glad to see you," Mrs. Lock assured her. "It would be awful if she got too nervous to go on."

Katie sighed. She was still really mad at Suzanne. But then Katie thought about what her mom had said. She and Suzanne *had* been friends for a long time. Besides, she didn't want Mrs. Lock telling her mom that she had refused to help Suzanne. That would make her mom really angry.

"Okay," Katie agreed. "I'll try."

# Chapter 9

Katie couldn't believe how crazy things were backstage. Everyone was running around, carrying clothes, hairbrushes, hairspray, makeup, and more!

The really little girls were with their moms. They looked kind of weird in makeup and grown-up hairstyles.

The girls who were Katie's age were all huddled together in one corner of the room. They were brushing their hair, zipping their dresses, and giggling nervously together.

The teenagers looked like real models. They were busy talking on their cell phones while they practiced walking in their high heels.

Katie looked around for Suzanne. She saw her sitting by herself in the middle of the room putting on makeup. Katie wondered why Suzanne was sitting all alone. Did she think she was better than the other models? Katie thought about walking away and leaving snobby Suzanne to herself. But Katie had promised Mrs. Lock that she would talk to Suzanne.

"Nice pants," Katie said as she walked over toward her.

"Huh?" Suzanne said, looking confused.

"I said, 'Nice pants,' " Katie repeated, pointing to the black leather pants hanging next to Suzanne's mirror. "They're really cool. You're going to look great in them."

"Thanks," Suzanne said quietly. She stared at herself in the mirror. "I don't think I can do this."

"*You're* nervous?" Katie asked her.

"I feel like there are a million butterflies in my stomach," she answered.

"You'll be great," Katie assured her. "But don't you think you should get dressed? The show is going to start soon."

Suzanne just sat there. Katie looked around at the other girls. They were all ready to go.

"Come on, Suzanne," Katie said. "You can do it!"

"Modeling is really hard work," Suzanne told her. "I don't know if I can be the best."

"You don't have to *be* the best," Katie said. "Just *do* your best."

Suzanne sighed. "You don't get it, Katie." She turned her head slightly and looked at the door. "Oh, thank goodness," she said.

"What?"

"My assistant's here," Suzanne said. "*She'll* understand what I'm going through." Suzanne stood up and waved her hands wildly. "Over here, River!"

Jessica ran over to Suzanne. "I brought your purple lip gloss," she told her.

"You're so great!" Suzanne exclaimed. She gave Jessica a big hug and leaped out of her chair. "So do you like these pants?" She held them up against her.

"They're awesome!" Jessica told her. "You're going to be the model everyone remembers!"

"Do you really think so?"

"Of course," Jessica assured her.

"Well, this *is* what I was born to do," Suzanne boasted.

Katie's cheeks turned almost as red as her hair. She was really angry. She had come backstage to be nice to Suzanne. But now that Jessica had arrived, Suzanne was completely ignoring her!

There was no way Katie was going to watch Suzanne's modeling show now. She didn't care what her mother had said!

Tears started forming in Katie's eyes. She didn't want to let Jessica and Suzanne see that they'd made her cry. Quickly, she ran to the other end of the dressing room. She saw a bathroom and ran inside. Katie locked the door so no one would bother her. Then she leaned against the wall and tried to stop the tears from falling.

Suddenly, Katie felt a cool breeze tickling the back of her neck. Within seconds, the breeze grew stronger, until it felt more like a wind than a breeze. And not just any wind.

*This was the magic wind!*

Before Katie knew what was happening, the magic wind was circling wildly around her. Katie grabbed onto the sink and held on tight. The tornado was really wild. Maybe the strongest it had ever been. Katie felt like she was being blown away.

And then it stopped. Just like that. The magic wind was gone.

And so was Katie Carew.

# Chapter 10

Katie opened her eyes slowly. She blinked a few times, getting used to the bright lights that were shining on her. There was a mirror right in front of her face.

"Oh, no!" Katie exclaimed as she looked at her reflection. Suzanne's face stared back at her from the mirror!

"What's the problem, Ocean?" Jessica asked her.

Katie gulped. How could she explain that the problem was that she *was* Ocean?

"I, uh . . ." Katie began.

"Five minutes, girls," a woman called out from the front of the dressing room.

"I'd better go get a seat," Jessica said. "You have to put those pants on. Isn't this exciting? In a few minutes, you're going to be a real model."

"Exciting isn't the word for it," Katie replied slowly.

As Jessica left, Katie stared at the black leather pants. She'd never worn anything made of leather! Katie was more into jeans and wool skirts. Leather was Suzanne's type of thing.

Of course, she *was* Suzanne now.

"Hey, Suzanne, you'd better finish getting dressed," one of the teenagers called to her. "We're starting to line up."

Katie sighed. She didn't know anything about modeling, other than what Suzanne had told her. There was no way she could go out there and walk like a model the way Suzanne did. She wanted to run away and hide somewhere until the magic wind came back.

But Katie knew she couldn't do that. This fashion show was really important to Suzanne.

And as mad as Katie was at her, she couldn't let her down. She was going to have to try and be Suzanne.

"Line up, girls," the woman in the front of the room called out. "The music's starting."

Katie quickly threw on the leather pants and zipped them on the side. Then she slipped on Suzanne's high heels and hobbled over to where the other girls were standing.

"Okay, ladies," the woman said. "It's showtime!"

# Chapter 11

As she waited backstage, Katie's stomach was doing flip-flops. She peeked out from behind the curtain. Yikes! The runway looked *really* long. She hoped she wouldn't trip and fall.

Katie watched the little girls parading in front of the audience. Desperately, Katie hoped the magic wind would come back. If it returned right now, Suzanne would be herself, just in time to go onstage.

But deep down, Katie knew that would never happen. The magic wind never came when there were people around. It only showed up when Katie was alone. And that

meant Katie was going to have to go out
there, in front of all those people, and model
the leather pants.

"Okay, Suzanne, it's your turn," the woman
who was running the fashion show said.

Katie took a deep breath. She lifted up her
neck and pushed her shoulders back, trying
to copy the way Suzanne had been walking in
the school yard.

Then she strutted out onto the runway. It wasn't easy, since Katie had never worn such high heels before. She blinked hard as the lights blasted right into her eyes. She couldn't see a thing. Of course, that was probably a good thing. Seeing the people in the audience would be too scary.

But she sure could hear them.

"Hey," one girl giggled. "That model is wearing her pants *backward*." The crowd of kids she was sitting with began laughing with her.

Katie looked down. Oh, no! They were right. The big back pockets were in the front. Katie had been in such a hurry to get the pants on that she hadn't noticed!

"Why is she stretching her neck that way?" someone else said. "She looks weird."

"Do you see the way she's walking? It's like she's on stilts."

Soon it seemed like everyone in the audience was laughing at Katie. She blinked

hard and tried to keep from crying. This was so embarrassing!

Katie knew she was supposed to smile. But she couldn't make herself look happy. She was too miserable. The high heels were starting to really hurt her feet. The lights were blinding her.

But as she turned around and headed back toward the curtain, Katie breathed a little easier. It was almost over . . .

*Boom!*

Just as she'd gotten back behind the curtain, Katie tripped over one of her high heels. The audience couldn't see her fall, but everyone had heard the thud. All of the models in

the dressing room began to laugh.

Katie's eyes welled up with tears. She stood and ran back to the little bathroom in the corner of the dressing room. Well, she *sort of* ran. Running is kind of hard to do in high heels!

# Chapter 12

Katie couldn't believe what a mess she'd made of things. Suzanne was going to be really embarrassed when she found out what had happened during the show. After all, nobody knew it had been Katie up there. Everyone in the audience thought it was Suzanne who was wearing her pants backward and walking funny.

*Suzanne was definitely the model everyone would remember.*

Just then, Katie felt a strong wind blowing through her hair. Katie knew right away what that meant. The magic wind was back.

The wind circled wildly around Katie. Katie

looked around for something to hold onto. Something that would keep her from being blown away. But there was nothing around. Katie shut her eyes and hugged herself tightly.

There was nothing she could do but wait for the wind to stop.

A few seconds later, the magic wind stopped. Just like that.

Slowly, Katie opened her eyes. She looked around. She was back in the dressing room in front of the mirror. But she wasn't alone anymore. Suzanne was standing beside her.

"Suzanne," Katie said. "Are you okay?"

Suzanne bit her lip. "Yes," she said. "I mean no. I mean . . . I don't know *what* I mean. Katie? What happened? How did I get here?"

Katie didn't know what to say. She couldn't tell Suzanne what had really happened. "Well, you were at the fashion show . . ." she began.

There, at least that was the truth.

"Oh, no!" Suzanne interrupted. "My pants are on backward."

"I know," Katie said. "But . . ."

"This is the worst day of my life," Suzanne moaned. "At least I think it is. I don't know what's going on. I mean . . . I was up on the stage, I think. And then I was back here again and . . . I'm not really sure. I'm so confused."

"You were just nervous," Katie said. "People get confused when they get nervous."

"I really messed things up," Suzanne said as she began to cry. "And lots of kids from school were there. They're going to make fun of me."

"No, they're not," Katie assured her.

"Yes, they will.

They'll all be happy to make fun of me.
Especially after I made such a big deal about
being a model." Suzanne gave Katie a funny
look. "How come you're being so nice to me?
I thought you hated me."

Katie shook her head. "I was mad at you.
But I could never *hate* you, Suzanne."

Suzanne shrugged. "Well, not everyone is
as nice as you, Katie. Jessica was out there,
and so were Miriam, Mandy, Becky, and Zoe.
I invited them. What was I thinking?"

"You didn't know that . . ." Katie began.

"I think I even heard George laughing in
the audience!" Suzanne sobbed. "I'm going to
be the joke of the fourth grade. I'm never
going to model again!"

"Don't say that," Katie pleaded. "You'll do
great next time."

Suzanne shook her head. "There won't be
any next time."

# Chapter 13

That night, Katie lay in her bed. She felt
awful. She might have been mad at Suzanne,
but that didn't mean she had wanted to ruin
her modeling career.

But that's exactly what Katie had done.
And what was worse, Katie knew Suzanne
was right. The kids in school *were* all going to
make fun of her.

And it was all Katie's fault.

Katie stared at the ceiling. There had to be
some way she could help her friend. But how?
There was so much the kids could laugh
about. Suzanne had been holding her head
funny and walking like a man on stilts. Worst

of all, she'd done everything with her pants on *backward* . . .

That was it!

Katie had just gotten one of her great ideas!

On Monday morning, Katie arrived at school extra early. She was wearing a striped pink-and-green sweater, and her new green corduroy pants. But . . .

*She was wearing the pants backward!*

Emma W., George, Becky, and Mandy were the first people to see Katie.

"Katie," Emma whispered to her. "Your pants are on backward."

"I know," Katie said proudly. "They're supposed to be that way."

The kids looked at her strangely.

"Suzanne wore them this way in her fashion show," Katie said.

Becky giggled. "I remember."

"It was classic," George added.

"*You* were there?" Mandy asked.

"I was on my way to Louie's," he said quickly, making sure the girls knew he hadn't gone to the mall to see Suzanne. "I passed the stage just in time to see Suzanne looking ridiculous."

Katie shook her head. "She wasn't ridiculous at all. That's the way all the big fashion models are wearing their pants now."

Becky and Mandy looked at her strangely. "Yeah, right. Anyway, we thought you were still mad at her."

"Well, that doesn't mean I don't trust her fashion sense," Katie replied.

"I think your head's on backward," George told Katie.

Before long, a whole crowd of kids had gathered around Katie. She was determined to make the whole fourth grade think wearing your pants backward was in style.

"You guys know Suzanne would never have worn her pants backward by mistake. She's too into fashion to do something like that," she told them.

"But your pants look weird backward," Miriam Chan told Katie.

Katie shrugged. "Lots of fashionable stuff looks weird. How about models who wear rings on their toes? Or male models who carry those man pocketbooks?"

The kids all looked at one another. It was

hard to argue with logic like that.

"I should have known Ocean was wearing her pants that way on purpose!" Jessica said finally.

"Well, I'm going inside to turn my pants around," Miriam declared.

"Me too," Emma S. said.

"I can't believe I wore a skirt today," Becky moaned. "I wish I had pants I could wear backward."

And then, Suzanne arrived. Everyone stared at her in surprise.

Suzanne wasn't wearing *her* pants backward. She was wearing a plain jeans skirt, a polo shirt, and flat blue shoes. She wasn't wearing any earrings, bracelets, or necklaces. She didn't have any glitter anywhere.

"Check out Suzanne," Kadeem said. "She looks so *normal*."

"Suzanne is never normal," Jeremy reminded him.

"Well, she *looks* it," Kadeem reminded him.

Katie felt awful. Suzanne without glitter was the saddest sight in the world. She hurried over to the bench where Suzanne was sitting all alone.

"Hi," Katie greeted her.

"Hello," Suzanne said in a quiet voice.

"You okay?"

Suzanne shrugged. "I guess." She looked down at Katie's green corduroy pants. Her eyes got really small and angry. "I can't believe you're wearing your pants that way. I thought you were my friend."

"I am," Katie assured her.

"Then why are you making fun of me?"

"I'm not," Katie promised. "I'm wearing my pants this way *because* I'm your friend. I

did it so no one would be mean to you."

Suzanne looked at her strangely. "Huh?"

"I told them you said *all* the top models are wearing their pants this way."

Suzanne smiled. "And they believed you?"

Katie nodded. "They figured if *you* were wearing clothes this way, it had to be a fashion trend." She pointed to Miriam Chan, Zoe Canter, Emma W., and Emma S. They had all just come out of the school building. And their pants were on backward!

Suzanne looked down at her plain, boring outfit. "But now everyone will know you were lying."

Katie frowned. She hadn't counted on Suzanne coming to school dressed like that.

Suzanne thought for a moment. "Unless maybe I . . ."

"What are you going to do?" Katie asked her.

Suzanne grinned. "You'll see. You're not the only one with great ideas, Katie Kazoo."

# Chapter 14

By lunchtime, most of the girls in the fourth grade were wearing their pants backward. But not Suzanne. She was still wearing her jeans skirt and plain shirt. Only the shirt wasn't so plain anymore. It had a big glittery *S* on it. Her pocketbook had an *S* on it, too.

"How'd you do that?" Katie asked as she stood beside her best friend in the lunch line.

"Glitter glue," Suzanne answered. "It was easy."

"How come you didn't put an *O* for Ocean?"

Suzanne frowned. "I think I like Suzanne better. It's a French name, did you know that?"

Katie smiled. "I like Suzanne better, too," she said.

Suzanne's glittery letters caught the attention of the girls in the fourth grade.

"Suzanne, how come you're not wearing backward pants?" Miriam asked her.

Suzanne sighed dramatically. "Backward pants are so last Saturday. Today, everyone's wearing initials. Check the fashion magazines. You'll see."

The girls all sighed. Once again, Suzanne's fashion trends were moving faster than they were. She was ahead of them again.

In seconds, there was a crowd of girls standing around Suzanne. They listened intently as Suzanne talked about how she painted the glitter glue letters on her clothes.

Katie moved out of the way and left Suzanne in the center of the crowd. She took her tray and sat down alone at a quiet table in the corner.

A minute later, she heard a familiar voice behind her. "Is it okay if I sit here?" Suzanne asked.

Katie looked up, surprised. She and Suzanne hadn't eaten lunch together in a long time. "Sure."

Suzanne smiled and sat down beside her. "Katie, I'm really sorry about being so mean. I guess I got kind of weird about this whole modeling thing."

"Kind of," Katie agreed. "But it's okay."

She paused for a minute. "I just have one question, though. How come you picked Jessica as your assistant and not me?"

"Oh, that's easy," Suzanne said. "An assistant works for you. But I could never be your boss, Katie. You're my best friend."

Katie smiled. Now she understood.

"I mean, I *hope* we're still best friends," Suzanne added nervously.

"Of course we are," Katie assured her happily. "You and I are friends *forever*!"

# Blizzard Fruit Salad

Suzanne and Jessica were at the next Cooking Club meeting. Here's the snack Katie and her pals made. Katie's mom did all the cutting. You should get an adult to help you with that, too.

**Ingredients:**

$^1/_2$ watermelon sliced the long way

1 cup cantaloupe balls

2 oranges sliced and peeled

1 large sliced banana

1 cup seedless grapes

$^1/_2$ cup pineapple tidbits

$^1/_2$ cup raspberries

$^1/_2$ cup blueberries

1 cup shredded coconut

1 cup oranges

1 tablespoon sugar

1 tablespoon cinnamon

**Directions:** Scoop out the watermelon half. Cut the watermelon into chunks. Combine the watermelon chunks and the rest of the fruit in a large bowl. Mix in the rest of the ingredients, except the coconut and cinnamon and sugar. Pour the mixture back into the watermelon shell. Mix the cinnamon and sugar together, and sprinkle it throughout the mixture. Then top the fruit with lots of snowy, white coconut.

**Here's what you do:**

Spread the newspaper out on a table. Use the pencil to draw a design on your sneakers. Here are some ideas:

- ✳ A shooting star like the one Katie wished on.

- ✳ A soccer ball—that's Jeremy's favorite design.

- ✳ Lightning bolts to show just how fast you can run!

Use the fabric paint to color in your drawing. Just remember, fabric paint is permanent. Once it's on your sneaker, it's there for good.

If, like Suzanne, you want to add some sparkle to your sneaks, try mixing some glitter into your fabric paint before you use it.

Okay! Ready? On your mark, get set, PAINT!